Her Third Queef on Mars

by

Ashly Gultz

This is a work of fiction. Names, characters, places, and incidents are products of the author's imagination or are used fictitiously. Any resemblance to real persons, living or dead, or actual events is purely coincidental.

For information about rights, permissions, or licensing, please contact:

xKotoba
www.xkotoba.com

ISBN: 978-93-47594-48-9
First Edition: February 2026
Cover design by: Saashi

xKotoba

xKotoba is for readers 18 and above—a space where love and desire are written in all their shades: tender, passionate, messy, and unforgettable. Each book explores intimacy and connection with honesty, from slow-burn encounters to bold, contemporary stories. These are books for late nights, quiet reflections, and conversations that linger. We publish fiction that goes beyond surface attraction, capturing the unpredictability of love, the ache of longing, and the strength it takes to stay. Relationships are written with depth, emotions with honesty, and every story reflects the complexities of human connection. For readers unafraid of love in its rawest form, xKotoba offers stories to be carried into the night, whispered about with friends, and remembered long after the last page.

www.xkotoba.com

Follow us on Instagram, Threads, Youtube & X
xkotoba

"Don't be gentle with me!" At her words, he dragged her around to face him, lifted her, and forced her legs around his waist. Three steps. A half-built bench. He dropped her onto it, not gently. The breath tore from her as he stepped between her knees, gripping her thighs, spreading them just enough to trap himself there. Her eyes were wide, lips swollen, body trembling with need. As her gaze met his, he thrust into her, ancient and inevitable. In that instant, she saw her desire reflected back at her. The world collapsed into heat and grip and want. The sound tore out of her, loud and wild. "God," he said. "Even when you fall apart, you ruin me."

1

She came apart just as the spaceship touched down.

The tremor of descent ran through the cabin walls, through the floor, and through her bones. It fused with the trembling already living inside her. Her breath broke loose from her throat in a sound she didn't mean to make. It startled them both. A soft, helpless, unfiltered sound.

Her second queef.

His mouth found hers instantly, swallowing the noise as if he could drink it into himself and keep it safe there. His hands were everywhere and nowhere at once, anchoring her to the present, to his warmth, to the fact that they were still alive, still together, still foolish enough to believe they could hide forever. She laughed into his mouth, half-shaking, half-crying. "That makes two," he murmured, his forehead pressed to hers. "Don't you dare count them," she whispered back.

The ship chimed. The landing sequence was completed. Reality returned like a slap. They scrambled apart, grabbing clothes, breathless, clumsy, still glowing with what they had done and what they could never admit. Their skins smelled like heat and danger and something almost holy. "UG floor. Cabin 7B," he said softly. "If we survive this." She nodded. "If Mars doesn't swallow us first."

He kissed her forehead once, reverent and quick, and disappeared down the corridor. She stood there alone for a moment, heart pounding, lips still burning where his had been. Then she touched her mouth and smiled like a woman who had already lost a war and decided she would keep fighting anyway.

It reminded her of their first encounter at the Launch Authority Hall.

It was early morning, but the sun had already burned white against the polished floors, throwing long reflections of bodies waiting to start their lives on another planet. The queue had curved like a quiet confession through the glass atrium. She stood with her hands folded at her waist, shoulders drawn in, a canvas satchel resting against her hip. Inside it were her credentials and a pressed flower from her mother's garden. The air smelled faintly of antiseptic and citrus. Everything about the place was too clean, too controlled, as if human longing itself had been sterilized at the door.

Mira Solene had trained for this moment for nine years. Nine years of labs, soil trials, simulated atmospheres, controlled famines, and endless nights staring at green things growing under artificial suns. She had told herself that this was what purpose felt like. That sacrifice should feel like this. Tight. Heavy. Important. And yet. Her chest felt strangely hollow. As if some quiet part of her had already stayed behind. The line advanced two steps. She followed, eyes still fixed on the transparent ceiling where cargo drones crossed like patient insects, ferrying supplies into orbit. Mars waited up there. The thought thrilled her and also terrified her. Made her heart beat too fast. Then she felt it.

A hand.

Not a grab. Not a brush. A nudge. A soft, unmistakable pressure at the small of her back, as if someone behind her had leaned forward and misjudged the space between them. Her spine went rigid. The sensation climbed up her nerves in a hot, electric wave that didn't belong to irritation at all. It was something else. Something intimate. Something wrong and right at the same time. She turned sharply, ready to snap.

2

"I'm sorry," he said at once. His voice was low, steady. Not flustered. Not defensive. Just… present. Her anger stalled mid-breath. He stood a little taller than most men in the line, broad-shouldered, hands already lifted in surrender. His hair was dark and unruly, like it had never learned to lie flat. There was a faint scar along his jaw, pale against warm skin. His eyes were deep brown, the kind that didn't rush. Watching her as if she were something he didn't want to startle. "I didn't mean to," he added. "The line moved. I forgot gravity still worked here."

A corner of her mouth twitched despite herself. "It does that," she said, more softly than she meant to. For a moment, they simply looked at each other. The world seemed to hold its breath around them. The murmurs of the hall faded into a low, distant hum. Her pulse thudded in her ears. She became acutely aware of the space between them. The shape of his mouth. The way his hands were still half-raised, as if he were offering peace. Then something inexplicable happened. Her hand lifted on its own. She didn't remember deciding to do it. She only knew that suddenly her fingertips were gliding along his cheek, following the faint curve of the scar. His breath hitched. Just slightly. As if he'd felt the same jolt she had.

A voice boomed from the front of the hall. "Next group forward. Microbiology candidates, prepare documents." Reality slammed back into place. Her hand dropped. Her cheeks burned. She turned away too quickly, heart galloping. God. What was wrong with her? She moved forward with the line, willing her body to behave, to be rational, to remember that this was not a romance novel, not a dream. This was the most regulated migration program in human history. Behind her, he followed. Not too close.

At first.

Then he stepped nearer. Close enough that she could feel his heat through the thin fabric of her jacket. Close enough that his chest brushed her back when the line stopped again. Her breath caught. The line shuffled forward again.

He didn't move away this time. Instead, he aligned himself with her, as if they were two pieces of a puzzle that had just discovered they fit. His hands hovered near her sides, not touching, but close enough that her skin prickled in anticipation of something she did not want to understand just yet.

She told herself to step ahead. Her feet didn't listen. When the line stopped once more, he closed the last inch of distance. His hands settled lightly on her inner thighs, fingers resting as if he were holding something fragile. A shiver raced through her. Her knees nearly buckled. Her breath came out in a sound she did not recognize. He stilled. "I won't," he murmured in her ear. "If you don't want this."

3

She should have pulled away. She didn't. Her body leaned back into his, fitting against him with a terrifying sense of rightness. Her head tipped slightly, exposing the curve of her neck without her meaning to. The world narrowed to the slow, hypnotic rhythm of his fingertips moving just enough to make her ache. It was madness.

It was everything. The space between her thoughts and her skin collapsed. She forgot Mars. Forgot rules. Forgot the years of discipline that had built her into someone serious and sensible. She only knew this: she had never felt so seen by a stranger in her life. He exhaled slowly, his breath warm against her hair. Someone behind them cleared their throat pointedly. The line had moved again. They were almost at the front desk now. A few curious glances flicked their way. Her rational mind clawed its way back. She turned, met his eyes, and shook her head once. A silent plea. A boundary. A warning. He lifted his hands at once. "Your word rules," he said, mock-saluting her with a grin that made her stomach flip.

She stepped forward, heart pounding as she had just escaped something dangerous and sacred at the same time. At the desk, a woman in a silver skin-tight uniform scanned her documents as she looked her over. The woman's generous curves were evident in her spacesuit, with its tight bodice and hip-hugging bottoms. Was she really a robot? Maybe she was cloned from a scientist's ex-lover, who had shunned his love, and this was his revenge. She also noticed the ample cleavage visible in the suit. "Mira Solene. Microbiologist. Agri-engineer. Dual-role clearance approved." The stamp hit the screen with a final, irreversible sound. Mira came back to reality with a jolt, her cheeks flushed because of her thoughts.

"Welcome to the Mars Colonization Initiative."

She swallowed. Behind her, she felt his presence like a promise she didn't know how to break. And somehow, without either of them saying it out loud, she knew this was not the last time their bodies would forget the rules together.

She did not turn toward the dormitories. The corridor ahead dipped into the service level, where the station stopped pretending to be beautiful. Pipes ran along the walls. The lights thinned out. The air smelled faintly metallic. She heard his footsteps before she saw him. Not hurried. Not hesitant. Just there.

She stopped. So did he. The silence between them was thick, charged, like the pause before a storm decides where to break. She turned slowly. He stood a few steps away, hands loose at his sides, eyes fixed on her as if she were something newly discovered and already impossible to forget. Neither of them smiled. She took a breath. Let it out. Then she stepped closer. The space between them folded in on itself. His breath changed first.

Her fingers brushed his wrist. A question. A warning. An invitation all at once. He did not move away. That was enough of an answer. She leaned in, resting her forehead briefly against his chest. The steady beat beneath her ear unsettled her more than the touch. She pulled him into a hidden service bay, and her mouth found his. Their lips brushed first, tentative, as if both of them were startled by how real the other felt.

Then she pressed in again, harder this time, hunger rising too fast for patience. His lips parted on a breath. She tasted him. Salt and warmth and need. Her hands came up to his neck, fingers curling into the short hair at his nape. He answered her kiss with a low sound she felt more than heard. His hands lifted, hovering for a fraction of a second at her waist, waiting. When she leaned closer, he took it as permission. His palms slid over her sides, slow and sure, thumbs pressing lightly into her ribs as if he were mapping her by touch alone.

Their mouths opened more fully now. The kiss deepened, not in urgency but in thirst. His lower lip caught between hers. She drew it in, gently at first, then with a little more insistence, a quiet ache blooming low in her belly. She breathed him in between kisses. His scent. Clean skin. Faint soap. Something warm and human beneath it all. Her tongue brushed his mouth. The sensual contact sent a visible shudder through him. His grip on her waist tightened, not rough, just suddenly more real, more claiming.

The station around them vanished. There was only the slow, aching rhythm of mouths meeting and parting. The soft pull of want grew heavier with every second they didn't stop. She pulled back just enough to breathe, their foreheads touching, mouths still brushing with every wordless inhale. Her swollen lips tingled. She kissed him again, slower now, savouring it this time. Letting the kiss stretch. Letting it say what neither of them was ready to put into words. Her body leaned into his. And she knew, with a certainty that made her chest ache, that this was not momentary. This was the beginning of something they could not undo.

4

His hands did not leave her waist. They moved up instead, inside her blouse, lifting it up, almost over her head. Slowly at first, like he was asking for permission. In response, she shrugged out of her blouse impatiently. He swore at the sight of her bosom in a see-through white bra. His palms slid up her sides with hunger, seeking the curve of her breasts, thumbs brushing their underside until they were finally holding her peaked nipples through the bra. Her hands tightened in his hair. Not gentle now. Needy. Her mouth found his again, rougher this time, all patience burned away. The kiss turned deeper, wetter, heavier with want. Their lips kept colliding, parting, chasing. He had unhooked her bra by then and held her voluptuous breasts in the cradle of his palms. He broke for air, and before she could claim his lips again, he dipped his head and kissed the luscious mounts. Her breath caught in her throat, and she bent backwards to accept his worshiping lips.

He took a deep breath, too, well aware of his growing hardness, now touching her yoni. He pulled her closer to settle her around his phallus. She gasped and clutched his buttocks. He started grinding into her, in rhythm with the kisses he was showering on her nork. Then, he took the left one in his mouth and sucked until she moaned. Her hand lifted the right one towards his mouth, wanting possession. He obliged. Caressing the left one with the tips of his fingers, he sucked in the right one, rotating his tongue around it. She moaned and moved her hands to his manhood. Touching it against his jeans. He responded by moaning and sliding his hands down her back. She made a soft, broken sound against his lips. He stilled for half a second, forehead dropping to hers, breath uneven. Her eyes were dark. Unsteady. Lit from the inside. She nodded once. Permission.

His hands moved again, bolder now. One slid along her hip, fingers curling into the band of her trousers, pushing them down. Then his mouth followed his hands. He knelt until he was facing her waist. She looked down, shocked, her hands tangled in his hair. He looked into her eyes with a hunger that burned her inside with want. Without breaking eye contact, he tugged at her trousers, let them bunch at her feet, and then attacked her skin-coloured panties. He kissed her through them, still making eye contact. She reddened and jerked by the jolt of electricity that swept down her thighs. He bent down and gently tore the piece of cloth to free a yoni already wet and hot with want. Then he started the brutal torture, circling it with his lips but not touching her core. Gentle fingers ran down her thighs and around her yoni, but never on it. She groaned in frustration and tried to push his head into her core. He laughed and resisted.

Finally, she could take it no more and hit his head. He reacted by plunging his teeth into her yoni. He bit it, ate it, and devoured it. She shrieked in pleasure, her hands and nails leaving their mark on his bare shoulders, which she had, by then, made free from its shirt. He caressed the bitten parts with his tongue, while his right hand moved up her belly to hold her left breast, not gently anymore, but with a passion that couldn't be controlled. She gasped and moaned until she could take it no more and pushed him away on the floor. He took her cue and lay down on the bare floor, while she mounted him. Two hands worked desperately to unbutton his belt and his jeans. She blushed when she saw that he wore no underwear.

In the next second, he pushed his phallus into her welcoming yoni. Her body felt as if it were dissolving into sensation. Every nerve too awake. Every inch of her skin was humming where his phallus touched her cervix. Her breath came out in short, helpless bursts. Her head tipped back, throat and bust exposed, mouth falling open as the pressure built too high to contain. Within minutes, they both came together, their union cemented with the first orgasm. As he took a deep breath to calm himself, a sound slipped out of her. Unplanned. Unfiltered. A ridiculous, traitorous burst of sound tore out of her chest, half-gasp, half-laugh, entirely out of her control.

Her first queef.

The moment shattered into silence. She froze. Her whole body went rigid, heat flooding her face so fast it made her dizzy. She tried to move away from him, hands flying up to cover her mouth, horror crashing through her. "I— I didn't—" Her words tangled and died.

He stared at her for one stunned second. Then his mouth curved into something soft and wrecked and utterly undone. A quiet laugh escaped him. Low. Breathless. Not teasing. Not mocking. Wonderstruck. "That," he murmured, cradling her face in his hands, gently lowering her to lie on him, "was the most perfect sound I have ever heard." Her eyes burned. "You are not allowed to remember that."

"I will never forget it." He kissed her again, slower now, deeper, as if sealing something fragile and real between them. She melted into him, embarrassment and desire twisting together in her chest. Her laugh came out shaky this time. She pressed her forehead to his. Neither of them moved away. And somewhere deep in the station, something irreversible had already shifted into place for a microbiologist and an architect-builder.

5

After three months of their first meeting, the spaceship carried them away from Earth like a held breath that never quite released. The launch itself had been a violence disguised as precision. A roar that swallowed thought. Gravity pinned her into her seat until her bones felt pressed into memory. Through the small oval window, she had watched her planet curve away from her, blue thinning into black, clouds dissolving into silence. Somewhere in that shrinking world were her parents, her old garden, the air that had shaped her lungs from birth. Somewhere in that same world was the moment she had met him, standing too close in a line that was supposed to change her life for practical reasons only.

The ship settled into its long-haul rhythm within hours. Artificial gravity stabilized. Corridor lights softened into a permanent twilight. The engines shifted from thunder to a low, constant hum that never quite faded, even in sleep. The Mars Vessel Helios became its own floating country, sealed tight and self-contained, with its population reduced to a few hundred specialists and thousands of quiet rules.

The rules were clear. Every colonist had signed the same clause. Emotional containment was listed under "Operational Stability Protocols," as if love were a structural flaw, like a crack in a hull. They were not settlers in the romantic sense. They were contractors of the future. They were builders hired before citizens were allowed to exist. The company called them 'First Phase Personnel,' a phrase so clean it erased the reality of what it meant. They were there to lay the foundation of a civilization, not live it. Every person aboard Helios had signed the same clause, buried deep in legal language but spoken plainly during the final briefing. No romantic relationships. No sexual contact. No emotional entanglements.

The company did not want complications. They did not want distractions amongst the workers. They did not want a human mess. They had studied Earth too well to pretend otherwise. Love led to loyalty shifts. Sex led to jealousy, attachment, and rupture. Pregnancy led to risk, liability, and delay. Even unmanaged desire led to irrational decisions. They wanted minds sharp and bodies predictable. They wanted workers who would see Mars as a job, not a home. Women were monitored more closely, their hormone baseline was recorded, and cycles were tracked under the language of health optimization. Fertility was treated like a malfunction to be prevented. Long-term contraceptives were mandatory and non-negotiable. Pregnancy was not forbidden because it was immoral, but because it was inefficient.

Men were cautioned in different ways. Briefings about focus. About how attraction altered judgment. About how attention, once redirected, did not always return to work. They were reminded that desire was chemical, manageable, a weakness to be disciplined.

Helios enforced this with architecture as much as rules. Separate quarters. Staggered shifts. Limited unsupervised time. Privacy existed, but intimacy did not. Cameras did not watch beds, but schedules ensured bodies rarely shared the same silence. Touch became accidental by design. A brush of fingers during equipment handoff. A shoulder bump in narrow corridors. Nothing that could linger.

At first, most personnel complied easily. They were professionals. Scientists. Engineers. Medics. Agritech specialists. Architects. They had trained for years for this mission. Mars was the dream, not romance. They told themselves they had left such needs behind on Earth. But the body does not sign contracts. Months into the journey, as Earth receded into abstraction and Mars grew heavier in the mind, something shifted. The rules did not erase desire. They sharpened it. Suppressed intimacy pooled in the nervous system. People became hyper-aware of each other, of voices, of breath, of warmth, in shared spaces.

Women felt it first, or spoke of it first. Hormones that had already been adjusting to microgravity began to behave differently under enforced celibacy. Libido did not disappear. It rerouted. Desire turned inward, vivid, dream-soaked. Menstrual cycles grew more sensitive to stress and isolation. Moods deepened. Emotions had nowhere to discharge except sleep, work, or thought. Men found focus harder than promised, not because of women alone, but because the absence of connection stripped the days of softness. Without intimacy, even platonic closeness, the work became sharper, harsher. Touch starvation crept in quietly, showing up as irritability, insomnia, and aggression that had no obvious target.

The company logs recorded productivity metrics. Output stayed high. Error rates remained acceptable. But something else was happening beneath the data. People lingered in shared spaces longer than necessary. Conversations stretched. Eye contact held. Small kindnesses took on disproportionate weight. A cup of heated water left outside a cabin. A tool repaired without being asked. These were not violations. They were symptoms.

Helios wanted workers. What it was carrying, against policy, and slowly, were humans on the edge of becoming something else. By the time they landed on Mars, the rules were still in place. But the bodies that stepped onto red soil were no longer the bodies that had agreed to follow the rules on it.

6

For the first two days on the ship, they pretended nothing had happened between them on Earth. They passed each other in corridors with the discipline of strangers. Eyes forward. Shoulders stiff. No pauses. No glances that lingered too long. No accidental brushes that could be read by sensors as intention. No shared smiles that might trip facial-recognition anomaly software.

And still, every night, her body remembered him. It remembered the weight of his hands at her waist. The heat of his breath against her neck. The touch of his fingertips on her nipples. The nibble of his teeth on her yoni. His presence had suddenly made the world feel unbearably alive. She lay awake in her bunk, staring at the curved ceiling panel where simulated stars drifted slowly past. The gravity felt wrong at night. Too even. Her muscles ached with the effort of pretending nothing had shifted inside her. She could feel him without touching him. In the way her skin prickled when footsteps passed her door, and her mind hoped, stupidly, that it might be his. In the way her breath caught every time she smelled faint soap and metal in the corridor air. In the way her dreams kept circling back to that moment in the enrolment queue, that first impossible alignment of bodies that had rewritten her sense of risk. She sighed in yearning and turned to her side, cuddling up to her bosom that craved another's touch.

During the day, she worked. She calibrated hydroponic systems. Ran microbial viability tests. Logged oxygen-yield projections. Argued gently with an AI assistant about nitrogen ratios and nutrient cycles. She spoke in clean, efficient sentences. She did everything right. So did he. She saw him from a distance in the fabrication bay, sleeves rolled up, hands steady as he supervised the assembly of modular habitat frames. She watched the way he spoke to materials, not people. The way he rested his palm briefly against a newly welded beam, as if checking its pulse. They never acknowledged each other. Not with words. Not with eyes.

Once, their paths crossed at a junction near the life-support ring. The corridor narrowed. The lights dimmed briefly for a scheduled power adjustment. For half a second, their shoulders nearly touched. Her pulse spiked.

The sensor in her wrist vibrated a quiet warning. He shifted his weight just in time to keep the distance compliant. They walked past each other like ghosts. That night, she pressed her face into her pillow and bit back a sound that had nothing to do with loneliness and everything to do with restraint.

The ship drifted farther from Earth. Messages from home grew shorter. Signal lag stretched conversations into fragments. Her mother's face froze mid-smile more often than it moved. The word "Mars" began to feel heavier than it had on the ground.

On the third night, she stood in the observation ring long after her scheduled recreation window ended. Earth was just a dot now. A memory more than a place. She wrapped her arms around herself, feeling small and enormous at the same time. That was when her wrist console chimed. One message. Unregistered ID.

UG floor. Service cabin 7B. Ten minutes. Lose all sensors.

7

Her heart kicked hard enough to make her dizzy. The ship hummed around her, patient and indifferent. Everything was still being watched. And still, she turned toward the underbelly of the vessel, toward the part of herself she had already failed to lock away. The held breath of the journey tightened and finally began to break.

The corridors were quiet, the kind of quiet that pressed into her ears. Artificial gravity hummed low beneath her feet. Doors slid shut behind her without sound, sealing off each decision she could no longer undo. Cabin 7B was unassigned. No cameras. No live sensors. A forgotten square of privacy floating inside a machine built to eliminate it. He was already there. He didn't speak when she stepped inside. He just looked at her. The way his gaze changed when it found her made something loosen inside her chest. Relief. Want. A strange, quiet joy she hadn't expected to feel this far from Earth.

The door sealed behind her with a sound that felt far too final. He didn't speak. He just stood there, watching her like she was something he had already lost once and wasn't willing to lose again. The air between them was thick. Pressurized. Almost visible. She took one step toward him. Then another. By the time she reached him, her pulse was so loud she was sure the whole spaceship could hear it. His hands lifted, hesitated, then settled at her waist as if he had finally run out of reasons to pretend he didn't need her. The touch was slow and grounding. Hotter than it had any right to be through layers of fabric.

She exhaled into his chest. Her mouth found his again. This kiss was nothing like the first. It was deeper. Hungrier. Possessive in a quiet, aching way. Their lips moved with a kind of urgency that had nothing to do with speed and everything to do with how long they had both been holding back. Her hands slid up his arms, over his shoulders, into his hair. She tugged just hard enough to make him groan into her mouth. The sound vibrated through her like a promise. His grip tightened at her waist. He pulled her closer until there was no space left between their bodies at all. She felt his phallus then. Unmistakable.

Solid. Wanting. Wanting her. Knowing it wanted only her made her knees soften. She made a tiny, helpless sound. His mouth left hers, trailing down her jaw and then her neck. He pressed his lips there, slow and open-mouthed, like he was trying to memorize her skin. Her head tipped back without her permission. Her breath fractured into uneven pieces. His hands slid up her back, pushing her jacket off her shoulders. It fell to the floor, forgotten. His palms followed, warm and steady, mapping the curve of her spine as if he were building something sacred out of touch alone. She shuddered.

8

Her fingers worked at the front of his jacket, clumsy with need. Buttons slipped through the wrong holes. She laughed breathlessly when she failed twice in a row. "Let me," he murmured. He caught her hands. Kissed her knuckles. Then undid the jacket himself, faster than she expected, as the restraint had finally snapped. Her hands went to his bare chest immediately. Skin. Heat. The slow, heavy rise and fall of his breathing under her palms. She pressed her mouth there, just once, just to feel the way his body jolted in response. His hand slid into her hair, not pushing, just holding her there like he couldn't believe she was real.

"God," he breathed. Her name followed it like a prayer. She climbed onto the narrow bunk without breaking eye contact. He followed her down. They didn't rush this time.

The pain of longing had made them patient. Patient enough to undress each other piece by piece, reverently, like every inch of skin revealed was something earned. As if to relish it in all its beauty and claim it with a humility that comes from knowing someone else controls your will. While she lay, he unzipped the inner vest of her suit, peeling it to reveal two magnificent orbs of beauty, caged in a gentle athleisure cover. He stopped for a second. Looking into her eyes, he revealed an emotion that took her breath away. A part of it relished it; the other part was scared, and it shied away from this commitment. She touched his phallus over his thin space tracksuit. He gasped and kissed her with all the restrained hunger of the past months.

She met the kiss with hunger of her own. While their lips joined, their hands found their own work; he pushed the bottoms of her suit down and away; her hands unzipped his pants and helped him shrug them off. Every brush of fingers sent sparks racing under her skin. Every new place his hands touched felt like a claim and a question at once. She arched into him when his mouth found her collarbone again. Her body was too awake. Too responsive. Every nerve was singing. She pulled him closer, legs wrapping around his waist, needing to feel all of him as well as the undeniable proof that this wasn't a dream she would wake up from. With their foreheads pressed together and breathing synced, for a moment, they just stayed like that. Hovering on the edge of something that felt too big to name.

She kissed him again. This time, there was no hesitation left in it. Her body took over completely. Her hands tugged at his phallus, guiding him to her yoni. Giving it permission to make her whole once again. He groaned and followed her direction, entering her with a long breath of union. His lips nibbled her breasts one by one, drowning them in sensations so wild and fulfilling that she moaned in pleasure. The rhythm of their union found itself without instruction. First, slow; then, desperate; then tender again. Each time, her hands clutching his buttocks with ownership, while his hands played havoc with her belly and her breasts. Mouths joining and plunging as if they wanted to know every single micron within each other.

Every movement felt amplified by the silence around them, by the knowledge that they were breaking rules written into the bones of this ship. Her breath came apart as she came first. Her body tightened around something rising too fast, too high. Her hands clenched his shoulders, the knowledge of the height she had reached breaking the tenacious thread his control was holding onto. He came, groaning in the joy as old as civilization, as ancient as conception. He kissed her mouth, laughing breathlessly into her lips as he held her through the aftershocks, his hands firm and gentle all at once. They stayed tangled together long after the ship's hum smoothed back into something ordinary. She looked at him, questioningly, "How did you manage to get an unregistered ID and keep the cameras away?"

"Madam, you are looking at one of the world's greatest hackers who ever existed!" he said, smugly. She laughed, surprised, "I could never imagine!"

He laughed, too, and kissed her hair, then her temple and her shoulder. Like he was afraid she might disappear if he stopped touching her. She made a move as if to rise, but he held her tight. "Stay," he whispered.

She closed her eyes. "I don't know how not to."

"Just tonight, stay." He whispered.

9

It wasn't just that one night. Since then, most of the nights in space belonged to them. They developed a rhythm. He would message first. She would always wait five minutes before replying, just to feel like she still had control. They met in different unused spaces. A storage bay near life support. A maintenance pod beside the water recycling unit. Once, dangerously, in her own cabin during a shift change when the corridor sensors were briefly down for recalibration. They learned how to listen for footsteps. How to freeze mid-breath when a drone passed overhead. How to hold each other in absolute stillness, mouths pressed together, bodies silent, hearts hammering, waiting for danger to move on.

Once, a security patrol paused outside the door. They were half-dressed. Her vest in his hands. His mouth still warm on her breast, and fingers plunged into her yoni. They didn't move. Didn't breathe. Didn't dare look at each other. The footsteps lingered. Then, they moved away. She pressed her face into his shoulder, shaking. He wrapped his arms around her and didn't let go for a long time. After that, the fear changed something. It made them softer, quieter, and deeper. They stopped just touching and started talking. Whispered confessions in the dark. About her childhood garden. About the way she talked to plants as if they could hear her. About his father teaching him how to lay bricks straight, even when no one would ever see the wall. About the loneliness of being useful but never essential. About the way Mars felt like a beautiful lie and a terrifying promise at the same time. Sometimes she cried afterward without knowing why. He never asked her to stop. He just held her tighter.

The night of the second queef had come without warning. They were reckless that night. Too hungry. Too loud. Too alive. They barely made it to the bunk before their bodies crashed into each other, laughter and breath and urgency blurring together. The ship shuddered as it began descent protocols. And she came apart at the exact same moment. The sound tore out of her yoni before she could catch it. Her second queef.

He kissed her mouth instantly, swallowing the noise, laughing against her lips, both of them shaking with adrenaline and delight and terror. They scrambled apart when the landing chime sounded. Space suits half-on. Hair a mess. Eyes too bright. They stood there for a moment, breathing hard, staring at each other like people who had just survived something impossible. "We're going to get caught," she whispered.

"Not tonight," he said. "Not ever, if we're careful."

She should have said this was over. She didn't. "We can't stop now," she said instead.

"I know." He said.

She said. "It's only going to get harder on Mars."

He said, "I know."

She turned to him. "Promise me you won't disappear." He took her hand. "I promise I'll find you. No matter how big that red planet feels."

She squeezed his fingers. "This doesn't end in orbit."

"No," he said. "It begins there."

They sealed it with a kiss. Outside the small round window, Mars waited. Red. Silent. Watching.

10

Mars did not welcome them. It simply waited. The ship shuddered through the final descent like a tired animal, engines coughing heat and fire into the thin red sky. She sat strapped into her seat, hands folded so tightly in her lap that her fingers ached. The vibration travelled through her bones and her breath. It also hit the fragile belief that she was brave enough for this. Beside her, separated by three seats and a rulebook thick enough to feel physical, he stared straight ahead. They did not look at each other. They did not smile. They did not touch. She felt tears burn her eyes without warning. Not from fear. From grief. From the knowledge that something permanent had just happened to her life, whether she was ready or not. The landing was rougher than the simulations had shown. A sudden drop. A sideways skid. The sound of metal screaming briefly against itself. Then stillness. The engines cut. The hum of the ship's systems softened. The cabin lights shifted from voyage-blue to colony-white.

A voice filled the space. "Welcome to Mars. Please remain seated until atmospheric equalization is complete."

She exhaled. The sound came out as a sob she hadn't planned. She kept her eyes forward. So did he. They disembarked in strict formation. Boots hit metal ramps, then moved to the sealed, pressurized corridors. Finally, they moved to the threshold of the primary habitat dome. The first thing she noticed was the smell. Not air. Not nothing. Something faintly coppery. Dry. Old. The second thing she noticed was the silence. Not empty silence. A weighted silence. The kind that presses against your ears and makes your thoughts too loud.

The third thing she noticed was the sky. A pale, dusty pink stretched endlessly above translucent dome panels. She stopped walking, *just* for a second. The line behind her halted. A supervisor cleared his throat sharply. She forced herself forward. But something inside her stayed rooted to that first step. The colony was still a skeleton. Half-built domes connected by narrow pressurized tunnels. Cargo crates stacked like temporary monuments. Drones were drifting through the air like watchful insects. Workers already moving with the dull efficiency of people who understood they were building history but didn't have time to feel it.

11

They were assigned quarters immediately. Separate. Of course. Her cabin was on the third ring, hydroponics-adjacent. Efficient. Sterile. White walls. A narrow bunk. A fold-down desk. One small oval window that looked out into nothing but red dust and scaffolding. Mars' sky was thinner than any blue they had known; a pale butterscotch haze stretched tight over a land that looked unfinished. Wind moved constantly, not loudly, but insistently, lifting red dust into low, looping spirals that scoured metal and skin alike.

Daylight was sharp and dry. Nights fell fast and cold, as if the planet exhaled and forgot them. They had landed in late northern spring by Martian reckoning, though spring here meant only that the sun lingered a little longer. Average temperatures hovered well below freezing. Inside the habitat domes, heaters ran continuously. Outside, suits creaked as seals tightened and joints resisted motion. Mars demanded effort for every step.

The first days were about survival, not wonder. Water was rationed, and so showers were a memory. The food was functional, packaged, and frozen. Sleep came in short, shallow spells because the planet's day was longer than Earth's, and the body did not adjust easily. People woke too early or too late, hearts thudding as if they had missed something important.

And slowly, without ceremony, Mars began to change them. The gravity was lighter, and the body noticed it immediately. Muscles softened despite constant exercise. Bones complained in ways doctors had warned about, but did not fully understand. Faces grew sharper, cheekbones more pronounced as fluids shifted upward. People looked faintly unfamiliar in reflective surfaces, like edited versions of themselves.

For women, the changes were more profound and more intimate. Within weeks, menstrual cycles began to drift. Some shortened, some stretched unpredictably. Ovulation became erratic. The body, sensing a hostile environment and reduced gravity, behaved as if reproduction were a risk. Estrogen levels fluctuated. Progesterone dipped and spiked without a pattern. For a few women, periods stopped altogether. For others, they came harder, heavier, accompanied by unfamiliar cramping.

Doctors logged everything carefully, gently, with professional calm. But among themselves, the women spoke in whispers about mood swings that arrived like weather fronts. Desire sharpened for some and dulled for others. Sleep brought vivid dreams, often erotic and unsettling. The mind, freed slightly from gravity's hold, seemed to roam further, faster. Skin grew drier despite humidity controls. Hair thinned, then stabilized. Nails broke easily. Breasts felt lighter, almost buoyant, which startled more than one woman the first time she ran on the treadmill.

Men noticed changes as well, though fewer spoke of them aloud. Testosterone levels dipped slightly across the crew. Aggression softened. Emotions surfaced faster. Arguments ended sooner, often in silence rather than shouting.

12

Mars was reshaping not just bodies, but also behaviour. Food became the colony's first true project because rations were never meant to last forever. The idea of livestock on Mars had once sounded like science fiction layered over logistics. But the colony planners had been stubborn visionaries. Embryos and genetic material had travelled frozen and protected, along with edited strains designed for low gravity, limited water, and recycled feed. The first animals were not animals at all, but life in vats. Cultured muscle tissue provided protein, bland but sustaining. It kept them alive, but it did not make them feel human. That came later.

The goats arrived as kids, small and oddly elegant, bred with reinforced bones and altered vestibular systems so they would not panic in low gravity. Their hooves were broader, softer, designed for synthetic flooring and compacted regolith. They learned to walk with a strange, floating grace, hopping more than stepping. The hens were quieter than Earth birds, their feathers denser to conserve heat, their wings weaker, but their bodies sturdier. They laid eggs slowly at first, shells thinner, yolks paler. The first egg cracked open on a stainless steel counter felt like a religious moment. People gathered without being asked. Meat came cautiously. No one wanted to be the first to kill something on Mars. When it happened, it was done with ritual care, a quiet agreement that life here had to be respected twice over. The goat meat tasted different. Leaner. Almost sweet. Chewing it grounded them in a way no protein bar ever had. Farms grew inside pressurized vaults, lit by artificial suns. The smell of hay and warm animals softened the sterile air. For the first time, Mars smelled alive.

And the people changed again. Regular access to fresh fat and protein stabilized their hormones. Menstrual cycles began to find new rhythms, not Earth-normal, but Mars-normal. Libido settled into something steadier, though often stronger than before. Touch became important. Not just sexual touch, but casual contact, hands on shoulders, bodies leaning close during long conversations.

The colony of workers built a culture that accepted that Mars would never be Earth, and that trying to make it so would break them. Instead, they allowed themselves to become something slightly different. Lighter-boned. Sharper-eyed. More emotionally exposed. More deliberate about intimacy, food, rest, and care. In the evenings, when the dust storms calmed, and the sky turned a muted rose, they would sit inside the dome, eating goat stew and boiled eggs, laughing softly, bodies drifting a fraction closer than intended. Mars had not welcomed them. But it was learning to live with them. And they, slowly, were learning how to belong.

They both changed, too, and took on additional responsibilities, wherever possible. He designed the living quarters differently after noticing how isolation worsened mood swings. Walls curved instead of forming harsh corners. Lights mimicked dawn and dusk more gently. Additionally, he helped the team rewrite work schedules to align with individual sleep patterns rather than forcing everyone onto the same Martian clock.

She fought hardest for the animals, arguing that food was not only nourishment but also a matter of psychology. That humans needed to care for other living things if they were going to stay human themselves. She documented the bodily changes with quiet honesty, refusing to sanitize the truth. She wrote about blood in low gravity, about desire in sealed rooms, about how women learned to listen to their bodies in a new way because old rules no longer applied. Together, they built more than a colony.

13

They learned each other's schedules without saying a word. The shift he worked. The corridor she took to avoid security drones. The maintenance junctions that were least monitored. The unfinished structures had blind spots where cameras couldn't yet see. Then, they waited patiently for the opportunity to touch, to kiss, to hold, or only to watch.

Days after their last meeting, she woke with an intense yearning for him. Her body craved his touch. Her shift began at 0600 colony time. As she walked to 'work', she noticed that the hydroponics dome was a glowing green globe, even though incomplete, in the middle of all that red. She stood inside it for a long time before starting work. The plants were still small and fragile. She had artificially coaxed them into being by her own careful designs, by placing rows of seedlings under filtered light, and cycling the drip of nutrient systems through pipes. Growing, nurturing life here on a planet that had never wanted it. Her throat tightened. She knelt beside the first row of oxygen-yielding crops and rested her hands in the soil medium. “I’m here,” she whispered. She worked until her hands were stained green and her shoulders ached.

After a tiring day, she didn’t look for him. She didn’t need to. She felt him like a pressure shift in the room. Like gravity recalibrating itself slightly wrong. That day, she saw him across the central junction. He stood near a skeletal frame of what would one day be a residential dome. Sleeves rolled up. Face dusty. His hands were steady as he directed a crew of three. Their eyes met for half a second. Not long enough to register as a violation but long enough to feel like an unquenched thirst. Her breath caught. His jaw tightened. They both looked away. That night, she lay in her bunk staring at the ceiling; loneliness hit her harder than the gravity ever had; she knew she was in trouble. She couldn’t imagine life without him now.

Their next meeting happened by accident. Or maybe it didn’t. She was inspecting a water recycling conduit near the edge of Dome Two when she heard footsteps behind her that didn’t sound like a drone. She turned. He stood there. Just him. No crew. No supervisor. The red dust outside the translucent panel turned the light around them into something warm and unreal. For a long moment, neither of them spoke. Neither of them moved. Then he said her name. Just once. Like he had been holding it in his mouth for days. Her knees nearly gave out. She closed the distance between them in three steps. They did not kiss. Not yet. She rested her forehead against his chest. His arms came around her immediately. Hard. Desperate. Careful. They stood like that for almost a full minute, breathing each other in, pretending the cameras were blind and the rules were imaginary.

“I thought you wouldn’t come,” she whispered.

“I didn’t know how not to.” He said, wrapping his arms around her as the warning of a dust storm blared over the speakers.

14

The dust storms were not events on Mars. They were seasons. At first, the workers mistook them for weather, as they understood it on Earth. Forecasts. Alerts. A few hours of inconvenience. They were wrong. A Martian dust storm did not arrive with drama. No thunder. No sudden darkness. It began as a restlessness in the air, a faint static on the horizon, as if the planet were rubbing its palms together. The sky lost contrast. Shadows softened. The sun became a pale coin behind gauze. Then the dust lifted. Mars dust was finer than flour, sharper than sand. It carried iron oxide that clung to everything: suits, seals, solar panels, and even lungs, if the filters failed even briefly. The wind speeds were not always violent, but the dust was relentless. It stayed airborne for days, sometimes weeks, circling the planet like a slow, choking breath.

During regional storms, visibility dropped to almost nothing outside the domes. The world turned the colour of dried blood. Inside, light dimmed as solar intake fell. Energy had to be rationed. Nonessential systems went quiet. The colony learned to live smaller. And then came the planet-wide storms. Those were different. The sky disappeared completely. Not dark, but thick. Claustrophobic. The sun vanished for weeks at a time. Temperatures dropped further. Static electricity built up in the airlocks, snapping at gloves and wrists. Dust infiltrated seals that had passed every test on Earth. Filters clogged faster than engineers had predicted. Everyone worked longer hours just to keep systems breathing.

Psychologically, the storms were brutal. People stopped going near the windows because there was nothing to see, and too much to imagine. Time blurred. Days felt longer, nights heavier. Sleep fractured. Dreams intensified. The human mind, deprived of horizon and colour, turned inward. Women felt it acutely. Hormones already destabilized by gravity shifts reacted sharply to the prolonged darkness. Melatonin spiked. Estrogen dipped for some, rose unpredictably for others. Periods stalled mid-cycle or arrived without warning. Moods deepened rather than swung. Desire turned inward, quieter but more insistent, like a pressure system with nowhere to go.

There was more touch during storms. Not always sexual, though sometimes it was fierce and urgent, bodies seeking grounding in other bodies. Mostly, it was proximity. Sitting close. Sharing heat. Fingers brushing wrists as they passed tools or cups. The storm made isolation feel dangerous. Arguments also surfaced more easily. Minor irritations grew teeth. The dust seemed to get inside people's thoughts, abrading patience. The colony learned quickly that emotional maintenance mattered as much as mechanical upkeep. Work shifts shortened. Communal meals became mandatory. Silence was discouraged.

Outside, the animals reacted too. The goats grew restless, stamping and pacing in their enclosures as pressure systems shifted. The hens laid fewer eggs during prolonged storms, their bodies conserving energy. Even the plants slowed, leaves angling differently under artificial light as if sensing the absence of the sun they had never truly known.

When storms finally broke, they did not end cleanly. The dust settled slowly, coating everything in a new layer of red, erasing footprints, softening sharp edges. The first clear sunrise afterward always felt unreal. People gathered instinctively, watching light hit the ground again, breathing deeper even though the air was still recycled.

After storms, bodies changed again. Menstruation often resumed abruptly. Appetite returned with force. Libido surged. People laughed louder, worked faster, and touched more openly. The colony marked storm-ends with meals that used precious fresh ingredients. Eggs fried in real fat. Meat simmered, shared generously.

Over time, they came to see the storms as allies. They learned their rhythms. Prepared earlier. Built systems that flexed instead of resisted. They adjusted their own lives to the planet's moods, understanding that Mars did not want to be conquered. It wanted to be endured. The dust storms became a kind of intimacy with the planet. A reminder that Mars was alive in its own vast, indifferent way. And every time the sky cleared, every time the sun returned after weeks of red blindness, they felt it again. The quiet, stubborn relief of being here.

15

After that one meeting, something had changed. The need to meet, heightened by the desire to just be around each other, became more desperate. That culminated in stolen moments in half-built structures, unfinished oxygen domes, and even inside storage tunnels waiting for sensors to be installed. They never stayed long. At first, they never did more than hold each other. They even learned the art of subtle glances and the language of passing fingertips. The way to stand just close enough in public spaces to feel each other's heat without tripping a proximity alert. They learned how to laugh quietly when a drone passed too close. How to freeze mid-breath when footsteps echoed. How to break away at precisely the right moment to look innocent.

The danger sharpened everything. Made every touch heavier. Every kiss deeper. Every separation ache longer. Their need for each other and the want of the other's body became sharper. His phallus throbbed to action only with a glance in her direction. Her yoni pulsated in recognition at his mere touch. As she saw him tease her core with the gentle rhythmic actions his hands made as he passed by, she thrust her breasts forward and unzipped her vest a little to show her cleavage. The sparkle of his eyes and the hiss of an indrawn breath were her sadistic pleasures, bringing a smile to her lips. With every gesture, every touch, and every smile, their desperation to love became a living thing. Alive and sustained by their passion and desire for each other. Until they thought they could no longer take it.

That's when the colony experienced its worst dust storm on Mars. The colony sirens wailed low and slow, a warning that the outside world had decided to remind them how small they were. All nonessential movement was suspended. Workers were rerouted into sealed zones. She sent the rest of the team ahead and stayed back to pause important experiments before catching up with them. But she found herself trapped in an unfinished oxygen garden dome near the perimeter. Just as soon as he heard it on the comms, he left his site and rushed to the dome.

The dome rattled softly as red dust slammed against its outer panels. The light inside turned copper and dim. He entered the dome and saw her standing there, alone. The storm howled. The world shrank. He walked to her and took her face in his hands. She kissed him like she was afraid the planet might take him away if she didn't. Their mouths met hard. Then slow. Then desperate again. Her hands slid into his hair. His arms came around her waist gently. She pressed closer. Needing the contact. Needing the proof of him. Her body reacted too fast. Too strongly. The intensity built like a wave she hadn't seen coming. She gasped into his mouth. He was kissing her forehead, her eyes, and her mouth with a tenderness that brought a lump to her throat.

Her head tipped back. Her breath shattered, and she pulled herself away from him. He frowned in worry, and his arms fell down, cold and bare. He looked at her with a query and hurt. Was it rejection? Had she found someone else? As he stared at her, she smiled, an almost devilish, evil smile. Then she walked a few steps back. Small, calculated steps, until she almost reached the dome wall. Lights flashed, and the dust storm grew louder and fiercer. "I don't want gentle and slow today. I want rough. I want to see how much you desire me. I want to see if you burn as I do." She whispered. She did not know she had it in her. He did not know she had it in her. This siren. This seductress. This woman, who drove him mad just by breathing.

She looked at him intently to see his expression. Would he mock her or reject her dominion? She didn't know him that well. But actually, she did. She looked into his eyes and saw the echo of burning desire she felt within her. He was aroused, his phallus clearly visible in his suit bottoms. His hands clenched in restraint. She had caused havoc with her words. Now he wanted to give her what she wanted and finally take her the way he had wanted when he first stood behind her in the enrolment queue.

16

Something in his expression broke. His jaw tightened. His breath changed. His hands curled into fists at his sides, knuckles whitening with the effort it took not to touch her yet. Not to take what she was offering like a man starved. "You don't know what you're asking," he said quietly. Her chin lifted. "I know exactly what I'm asking."

The storm outside the dome screamed against the panels, red dust battering the glass as if the planet itself were furious with them. He took one step toward her. Then another. She didn't move. Didn't retreat. Didn't soften her gaze. She stood there like a challenge. "You want to see if I burn," he said, voice low and raw. "You want proof."

"Yes." The word fell from her mouth like a blade. That was it. He closed the distance in two strides. His hands came up fast, gripping her hips hard enough to make her gasp. Not gentle, only claiming. He lifted her just enough to slam her back against the curved glass wall of the dome, the impact rattling through her spine and tearing a sharp breath out of her. Her eyes went wide. Then dark.

Then she laughed—a broken, breathless sound that only fuelled him more. His mouth crashed into hers. Not a kiss. A collision. Teeth scraped. Lips bruised. Breath stolen. His tongue forced its way past her lips like he had no intention of asking permission ever again. Her hands flew into his hair, yanking him closer instead of pushing him away. His hands got busy unzipping and throwing her suit vest away. Free from all constraints, her back arched off the glass as he kissed her neck and her bust like he meant to ruin her memory of every other man who had ever touched her. Her bosom responded by thrusting out, nipples perked, inviting his lips for more. He crushed them, sucked them in until her moans vibrated in the dome, bouncing off the walls, and competing with the storm.

She was still moaning when his hands slid down her sides, gripping her thighs, dragging her leg up around his waist. The movement was abrupt. Dominant. A command disguised as touch. He let her go a minute to push down his suit's bottom first and then hers. As they joined at the waist, she let out a low, helpless, wrecked groan. Her nails dug into his shoulders. "God," she breathed. "Yes." The way she said it almost undid him. He pressed his forehead to hers, breath coming hard and uneven, eyes blown dark with want. "You have no idea what you do to me," he said. "No idea how long I've wanted to do this to you."

"Then stop holding back."

That was his last thread of restraint snapping. He spun her around, pinning her chest-first against the glass this time. One hand braced beside her head. The other slid down her back, gripping her hip hard enough to leave fingerprints later. She gasped. Her breath fogged the panel. The storm outside roared louder, as if answering them. "You like being wanted like this," he said roughly. "Don't you?"

"Yes," she whispered, shaking. He kissed her neck hard enough to make her cry out. Bit her shoulder. Licked the sting away. His body pressed into hers from behind, undeniable, relentless, making it impossible for her to forget how badly he wanted her. Her thighs trembled. Her breath shattered into helpless little sounds. Her body was too awake. Too open. Too desperate for the friction he was denying her. He murmured. "You said one sentence, and you turned me into this." His hand slid around her waist, splaying over her stomach, holding her still while his mouth kept working her neck, her jaw, her ear. He whispered. "You want to feel it?"

17

"Yes," she sobbed. He dragged her back around to face him, lifting her again, forcing her legs to wrap around his waist as he carried her three steps to a half-built bench and dropped her onto it. Not gently. She bounced once, breath leaving her in a sharp gasp. He stepped between her knees immediately, gripping her thighs, spreading them just enough to cage himself there. Her eyes were blown wide. Her body was shaking with need. He kissed her again, brutal and devouring, pouring every day of restraint, every night of hunger, every second of fear into that kiss. His hands pinned her wrists above her head against the bench. That's when he pulled her face to look into her eyes. Just as she did, he plunged his phallus into her yoni, as old as time. In that instant, she saw the love and desire she felt mirrored in his.

As he thrust deeper, her yoni came to envelop his manhood with its juices. Her body arched up into him.

Her breath came apart. She was burning. He was burning. The storm screamed. The dome rattled. The world narrowed to heat and grip and mouth, and to the quiet violence of how badly they wanted each other. And then she lost control of the sound. It ripped out of her without warning. Loud. Broken. Wild.

Her third queef.

It echoed off the glass and metal and vanished into the storm outside. She froze in horror. He stared at her and laughed—wrecked, breathless, feral laughter. "God," he said. "Even when you come apart, you ruin me."

She collapsed forward into his chest, shaking, laughing, and crying at the same time. "I cannot believe you made me do that." He wrapped his arms around her hard, crushing her against him like he was afraid the planet might steal her if he let go. "You told me to be rough," he murmured into her hair. "You have no idea how much I still held back." She smiled weakly against his chest. "Next time," she whispered. His grip tightened. "There will be a next time."

Relieved. Delighted. He pulled her into his chest and held her there while her body trembled through the aftermath.

"I think Mars just officially knows we're in love," he murmured. She buried her face into his shoulder, mortified and undone and completely wrecked with relief. The storm began to fade.

The danger didn't.

They were almost caught three days later. They were meeting in a half-built residential dome when a maintenance drone rerouted unexpectedly. The sensor grid came online early. Lights flared. The door seal hissed. They had seconds. She dove behind a structural pillar. He flattened himself against a scaffold beam. Their hearts pounded so loud she was sure the drone could hear them. The machine hovered. Scanned. Paused. Her wrist console vibrated a silent warning. Then, mercifully, the drone drifted away. They didn't move for a full minute after it left. When they finally came back together, their hands were shaking. "This has to stop," she whispered.

"I know." He replied.

Neither of them meant it.

"If we get caught—" she asked. He replied, "I know." She closed her eyes.

"We're not stopping." She asked. "No," he replied.

They kissed again. Not reckless. Not desperate. A vow.

Outside, Mars stretched endlessly red and silent. Inside, two humans were quietly writing the planet's first love story.

to be continued...

www.ingramcontent.com/pod-product-compliance
Lightning Source LLC
Chambersburg PA
CBHW062147160726
48282CB00027B/955
* 9 7 8 9 3 4 7 5 9 4 4 8 9 *